Pat Hutchins

MULBERRY BOOKS • New York

Inquiries should be addressed to Greenwillow Books,
William Morrow and Company, Inc.,
1350 Avenue of the Americas, New York, N.Y. 10019.
Printed in the United States of America
3 4 5 6 7 8 9 10
First Mulberry Edition, 1989.

Library of Congress Cataloging in Publication Data
Hutchins, Pat (date) Don't forget the bacon!
SUMMARY: A little boy goes grocery shopping for his mother
and tries hard to remember her instructions.
[1. Stories in rhyme]   I.   Title.   PZ8.3.H965Do   [E]
75-17935   ISBN 0-688-80019-X   ISBN 0-688-84019-1 lib. bdg.
ISBN 0-688-06787-5 (1987 Printing)   ISBN 0-688-06788-3 (lib. bdg. 1987 Printing)

For Ben and Jeb Kidd

a cape for me?